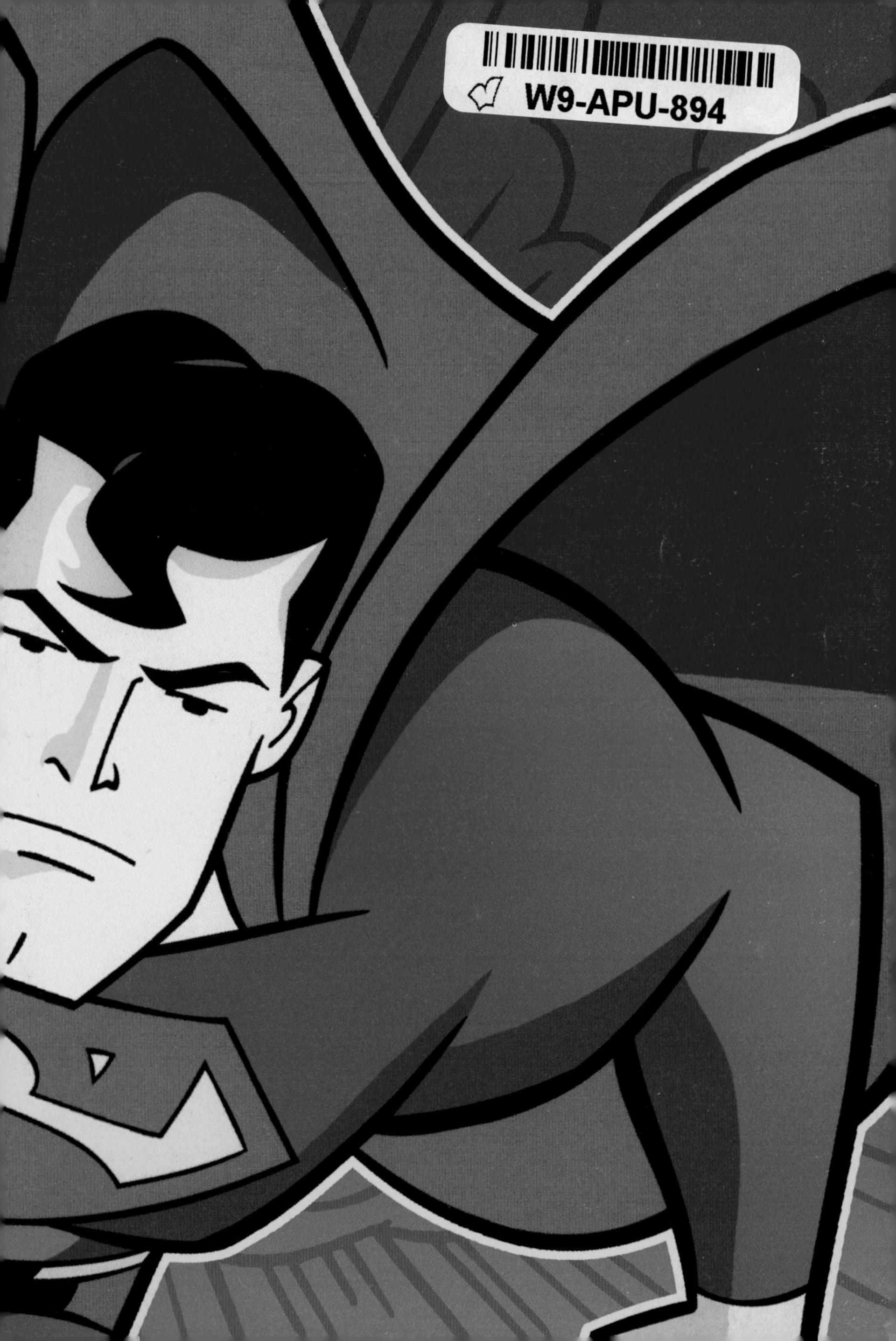

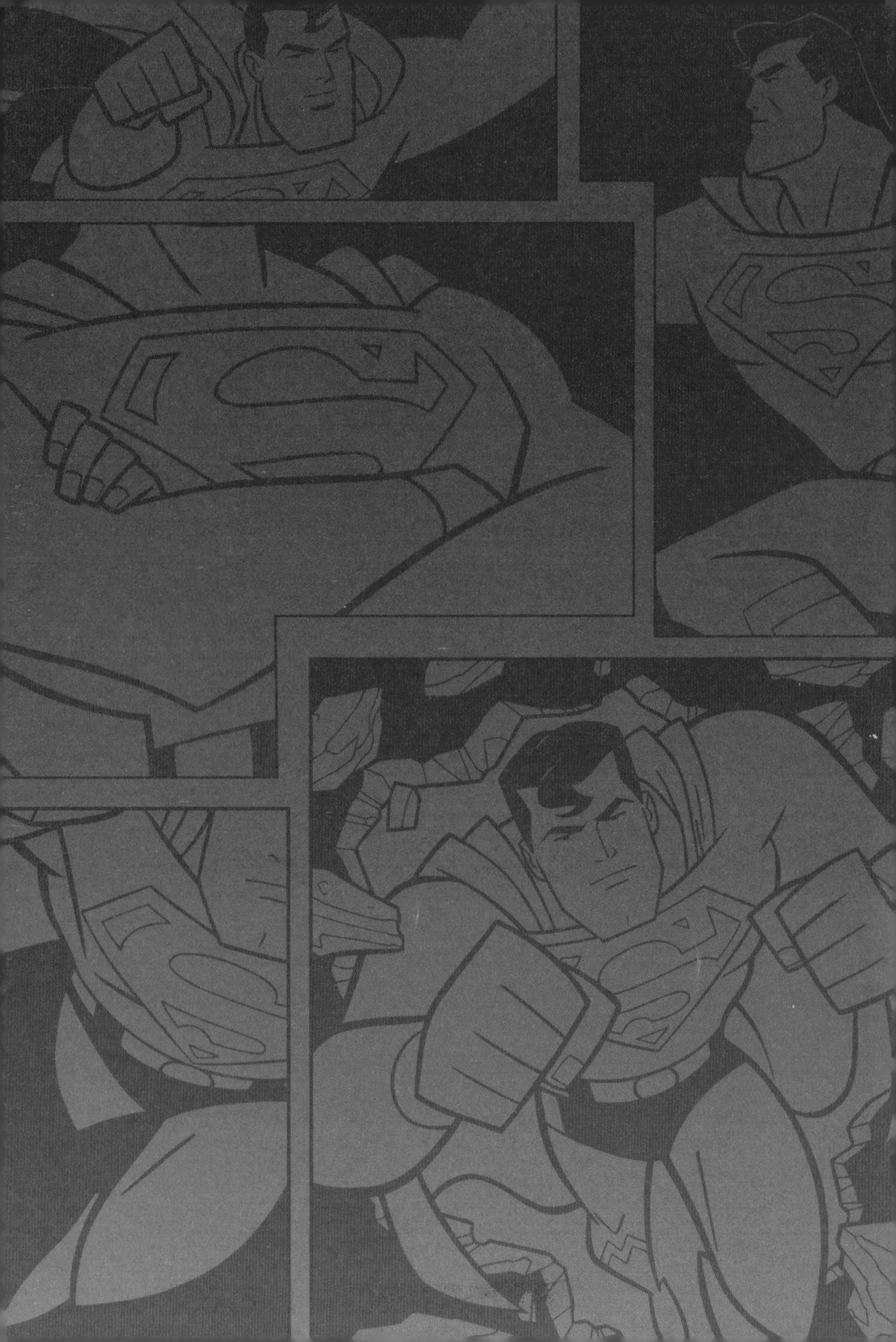

SUPER DC HEROES

SUPERMAN

PRANKSTER
OF PRIME TIME

WRITTEN BY
MARTIN PASKO

ILLUSTRATED BY
RICK BURCHETT AND
LEE LOUGHRIDGE

SUPERMAN CREATED BY
JERRY SIEGEL AND
JOE SHUSTER

STONE ARCH BOOKS
a capstone imprint

Published by Stone Arch Books in 2011
A Capstone Imprint
151 Good Counsel Drive, P.O. Box 669
Mankato, Minnesota 56002
www.capstonepub.com

Cataloging-in-Publication Data available on the Library of Congress
website.

ISBN: 978-1-4342-1986-2 (library binding)
ISBN: 978-1-4342-2763-8 (paperback)

Summary: After being released from prison, the evil Prankster vows to
turn over a new leaf. Instead of using his trickster talents for trouble, he's
taking them to TV. As the host of a new show, the villain recruits teens
to perform practical jokes. At first, the show is a hit. Soon, however, each
prank becomes a preview for a crime, and Superman isn't amused. He's
sending teen reporter Jimmy Olsen to investigate and stop this reality show
from becoming a real-life disaster.

Art Director: Bob Lentz
Designer: Hilary Wacholz
Production Specialist: Michelle Biedscheid

Printed in the United States of America in Stevens Point, Wisconsin.
072011
006313R

TABLE OF CONTENTS

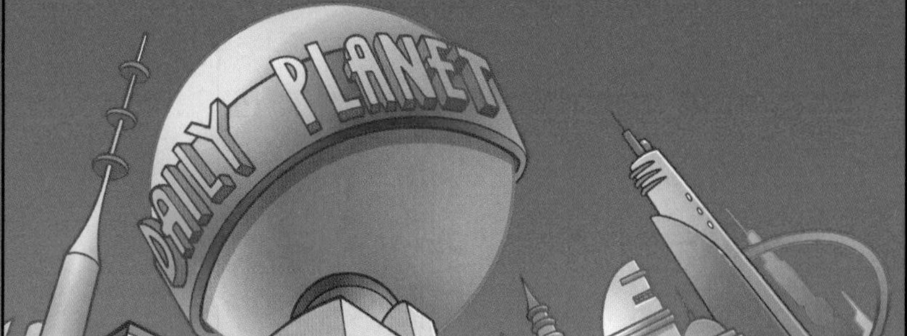
DAILY PLANET

CHAPTER 1

CAR TROUBLE

WHOOOOSH! Superman soared above the city of Metropolis. He was flying overhead on his regular patrol, looking downward with his super-vision. This superpower allowed him to see faraway objects as if they were just a few feet away.

As he scanned the city with his X-ray vision, he spotted three suspicious men inside a luxury car dealership. Each of them was trying to break into an expensive vehicle. One was picking the lock of a gigantic SUV. Another had smashed a window of a high-priced sedan.

The third crook was already behind the wheel of a German sports car that had shiny rims and a custom paint job. He was attempting to hot-wire the vehicle.

Superman landed inside the dealership. Immediately, all three burglars panicked. They ran for the door.

Without hesitating, the Man of Steel stomped his foot on the floor. **THUD!** The force of the stomp made the whole building shake. **RUMMMMMMMMBLE!** The crooks tripped and fell before they could reach the exit.

As the men struggled to their feet, Superman grabbed hold of the gigantic SUV. He opened the rear doors and then effortlessly pushed the vehicle toward them. **SKREEE-EEE-EEECH!**

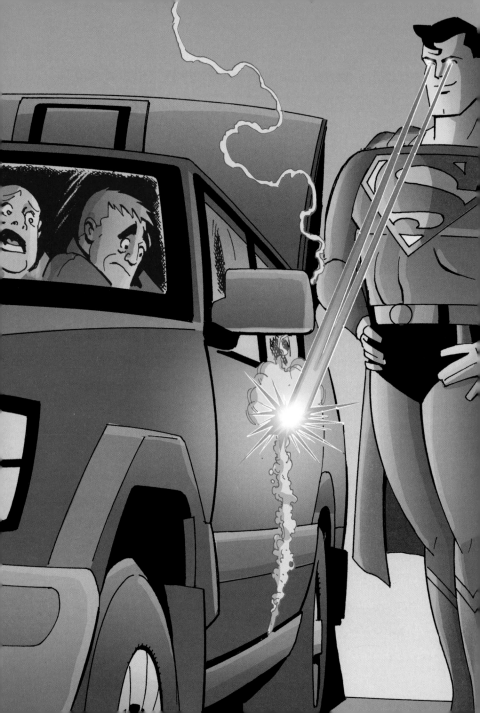

The open rear end of the SUV swallowed two of the crooks, and then slid into place against the wall. Neither of the men were hurt, but now they were trapped in the back of the SUV!

Superman made sure they couldn't escape by melting the locks with his heat vision. *BZZT!*

Meanwhile, the third burglar had released the emergency brake on another vehicle. It was rolling toward a chair near the corner of the showroom. Just then, Superman noticed a security guard sitting in the chair! The crooks had tied him to it with plastic cord and put tape over his mouth.

Superman leaped between the guard and the car, gently stopping it with his super-strong hands.

While Superman had been saving the guard, the third crook had vanished from sight.

The Man of Steel ripped through the heavy cord that bound the guard. **SNAP!** The plastic split in half as if it were a rubber band.

Superman gently removed the tape from the man's mouth. "Are you okay?" asked the Man of Steel.

"I think so," the guard replied. "Thanks, Superman!"

BARROOOOOMMM! The sound of a siren meant the police had arrived.

The super hero slowly pulled the SUV away from the wall. The two crooks shot Superman a nervous glance and stayed put inside the back of the SUV.

The police swarmed into the showroom, led by Lieutenant Dawn Valens.

She glanced inside the SUV and smiled. "You always come up with such interesting ways of catching criminals, Superman," she said with a smile.

"I'm afraid the third criminal escaped," Superman told her. "I can't find any trace of him."

"Don't worry, Superman," Lieutenant Valens said. "We'll catch him eventually."

Superman scanned the floor with his X-ray vision. Beneath the dealership's showroom, he saw a hole the men had dug. A tunnel beneath the building opened into its basement and entered the dealership from underground! Superman informed the police about the tunnel.

In the blink of an eye, Superman moved the cars back into their places and repaired the damage done to the SUV's locks.

Then, he flew toward the Daily Planet Building. Suddenly, his super-hearing picked up an excited voice talking about a practical joke. It was a voice he had hoped he would never hear ever again. A voice that meant just one thing — trouble!

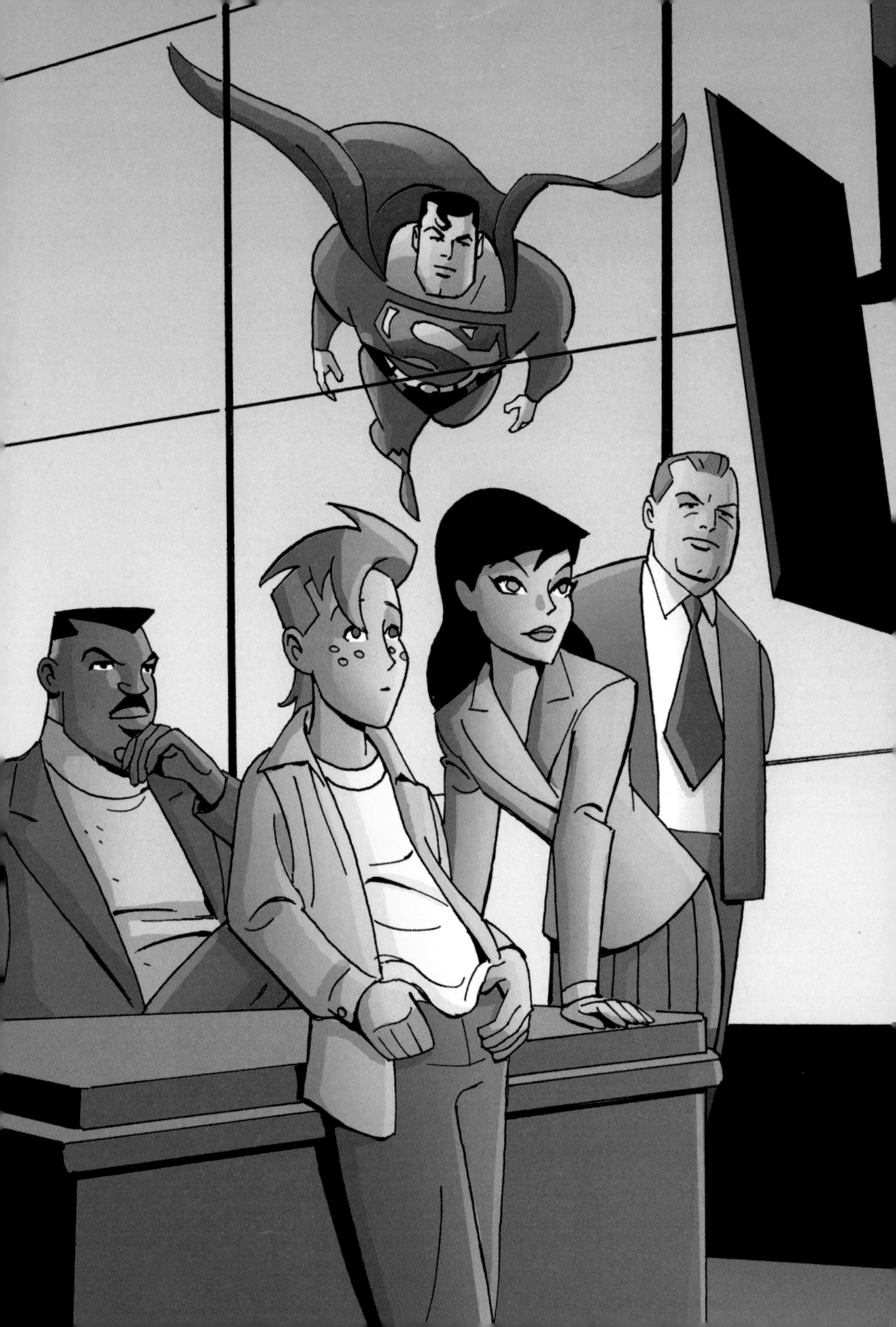

The familiar voice stopped talking as
Superman landed on the Daily Planet
Building's rooftop. He stepped into the
stairwell to change into his Clark Kent
clothes. He kept his X-ray vision and super-
hearing trained on the TV.

A small crowd stood around one of
the TV monitors normally tuned to news
channels. Clark's friends, reporter Lois
Lane, and the *Daily Planet*'s teenaged
photographer, Jimmy Olsen, were there.
They were watching *Gotcha!*

Gotcha! was the most successful new reality show on TV. It showed people pulling pranks on each other. The host was a hot new star named Alex Ryan.

Suddenly, editor-in-chief Perry White started yelling. "What are you people doing?" he shouted. "It certainly doesn't look like work!" The other reporters scurried back to their desks. Only Jimmy and Lois remained in front of the TV.

"Check this out, Chief!" Jimmy said, pointing to the television.

The screen showed a convenience store that was a total mess. Customers were slipping and sliding on the floor, which was covered in a deep puddle of bright red slush. A teen behind the counter was trying to turn off the "Shmushie" drink machine, but the button didn't work.

Nothing could stop the streams of Shmushie that kept oozing onto the floor, over the countertops, everywhere!

"This show rocks!" Jimmy said, laughing. "Alex Ryan is a genius!"

"You mean all this is being done on purpose?" asked Perry White.

"Sure," Jimmy said. "Kids try out for the show, and if they get picked, they get to prank their friends on TV!"

The face of Alex Ryan appeared on the screen. He continued explaining what was happening in the store.

"Darren's co-workers got tired of him leaving a mess every time he made a Shmushie," Ryan said. "So, they rigged the machine to make the biggest mess of all! Maybe now he's learned his lesson!"

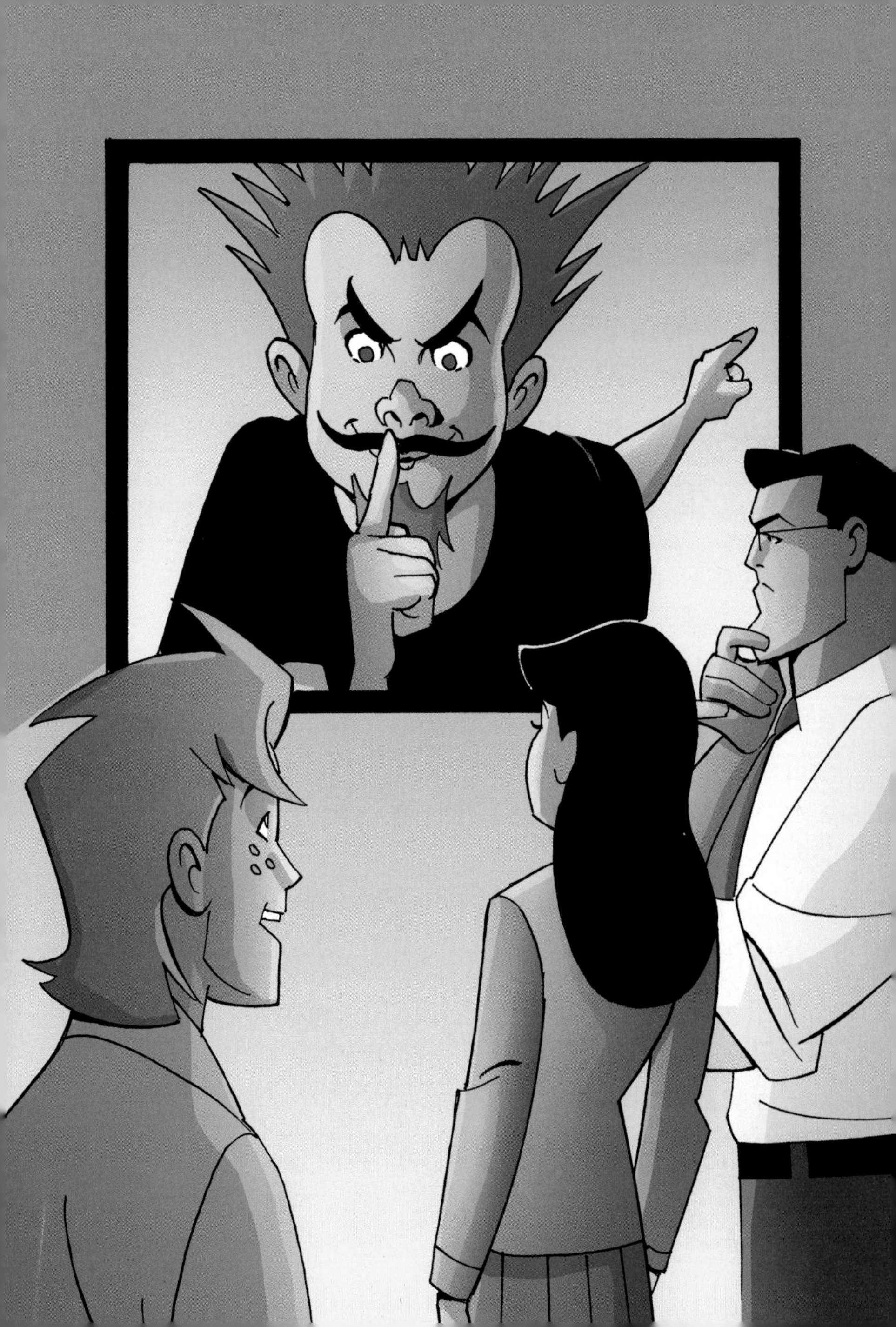

"That's hilarious!" Jimmy said, letting out another laugh. "Best host ever!"

Lois noticed Ryan's spiky hair, goatee, and bright white teeth seemed a little *too* perfect. "This Alex Ryan guy looks kind of familiar," she said. "And why's he talking so strangely?"

Clark stepped out of the room. He was trying to focus on something. His super-hearing was able to identify suspects from recordings, even when they tried to disguise their voices. Clark could tell that Ryan was using a fake voice.

In the news room, Perry White switched off the TV set and stomped back into his office. "Back to work!" he shouted.

THUD! The walls shook as the door slammed behind him.

Lois turned to see Clark Kent come back into the room. "I was just talking to Superman," Clark said. "You were right about Alex Ryan, Lois. Superman thinks he's really Oswald Loomis in disguise."

Lois's eyes widened. "You mean Superman's old enemy, the Prankster?" she asked.

"That's right," said Clark. "He was recently released from jail."

Jimmy chuckled. "Then he's found the perfect way to go straight," he said. "Now he can prank people and get paid for it!"

Clark wasn't so sure. "If a guy like that wanted to go straight, he would've done it a long time ago," he said.

Jimmy knew what Clark meant. Oswald Loomis wasn't just mean, he was crazy.

He couldn't keep himself from pulling pranks. Not even psychiatrists could help him. What's worse — his pranks almost always led to people getting hurt.

Lois shook her head. "That doesn't prove he's up to something," she said. "We need hard evidence."

"You know," Jimmy said, "the show uses kids my age. This is my chance to show the Chief that I can do more than just snap photos!"

"What do you mean?" Lois asked, looking confused.

"I'm going to be an investigative reporter just like you guys," Jimmy said excitedly. "I'm going undercover!"

"Wait, Jimmy," Clark said. "That's too dangerous. You don't have any training!"

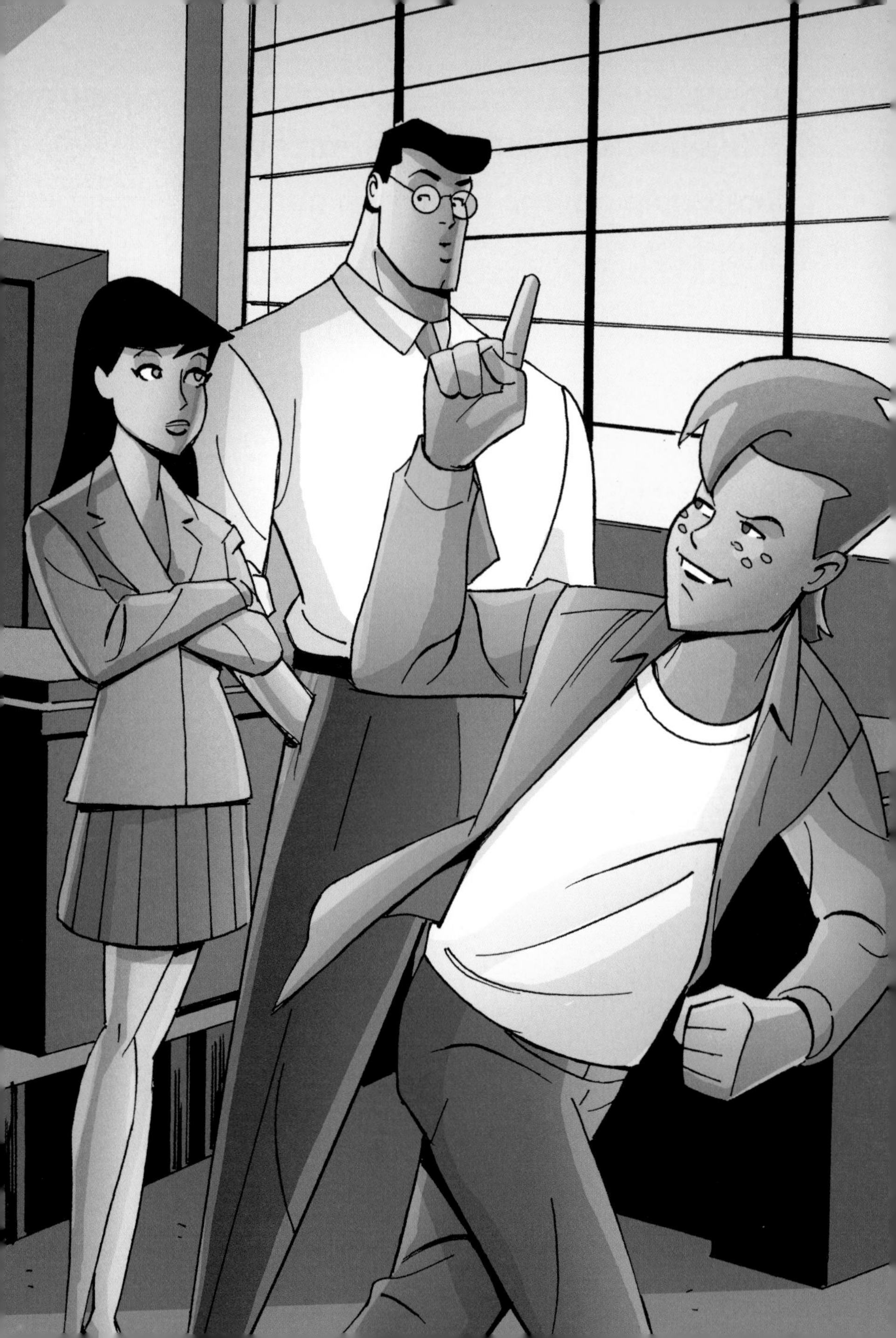

But it was too late. Jimmy ran out the door before anyone could stop him.

Clark and Lois exchanged nervous glances. Now, they had something more than just the Prankster to be worried about!

CHAPTER 3

MEET BART ALTON

In the production offices of *Gotcha! Studios*, a teenager with black hair and glasses was doing a magic trick. He made a coin disappear from the palm of his hand as the cameraman taped it. Alex Ryan stood nearby, watching very closely.

"You've got talent, Bart," said Kayla, the show's producer. "And you look great on camera." She was watching him on a monitor and taking notes.

Bart Alton, of course, was really James Bartholomew Olsen in disguise.

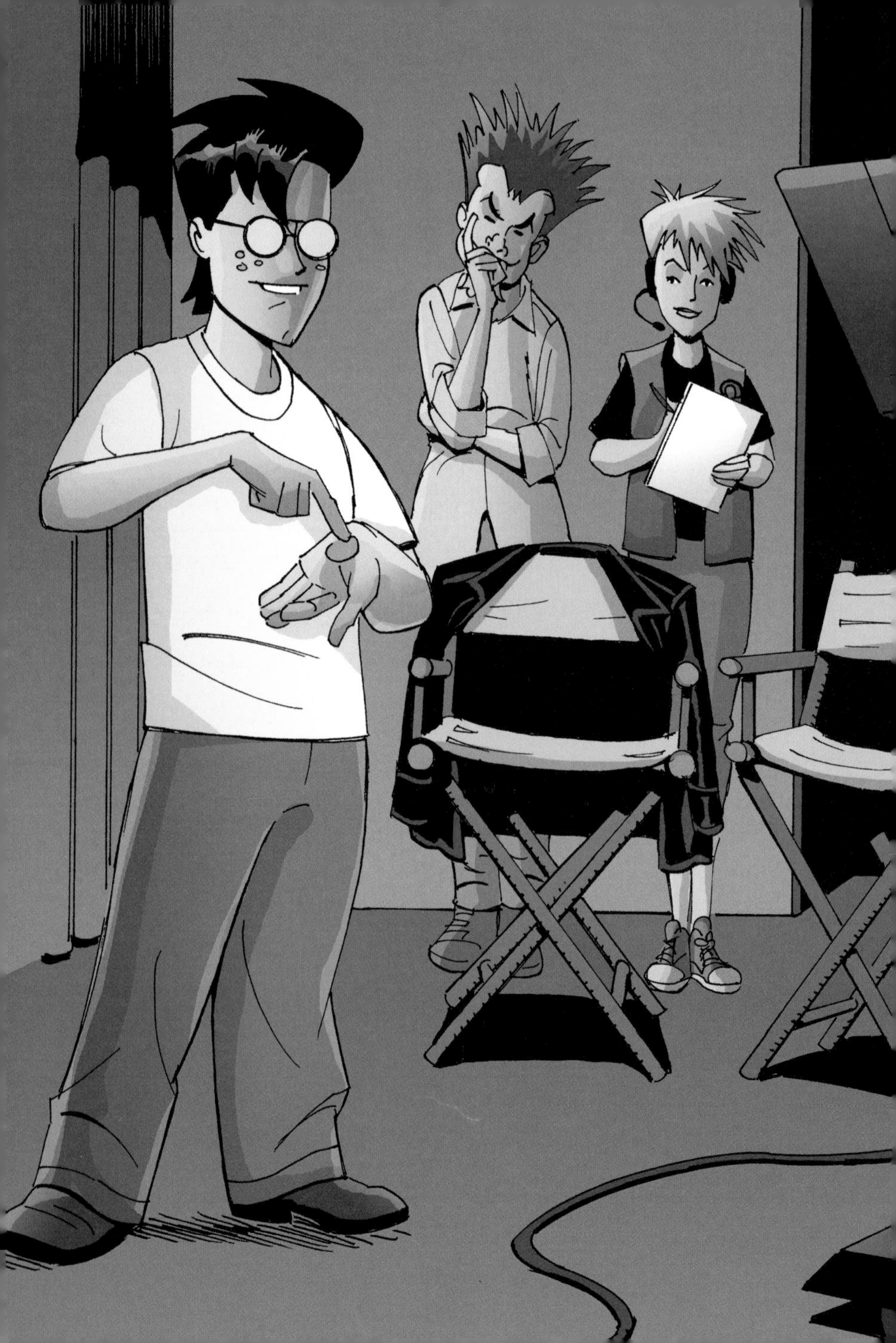

Jimmy was wearing a black wig and a pair of fake glasses to complete his disguise.

Kayla dismissed the cameraman, then turned to Jimmy. "Be back here tomorrow morning at ten," she said. "We'll use you for one of our shows."

Jimmy let out a cheer of victory. "I can't wait!" he shouted. The boy grabbed his jacket off the back of a chair and dashed off. "See you tomorrow," he said, closing the door behind him.

Out in the empty hall, he saw a sign for the exit. Instead, he headed in the opposite direction. The sight of a vent on the wall had given him an idea.

Back in the studio, Ryan was standing just behind the chair where Jimmy had hung his jacket during his tryout.

"Let's use him for the car prank," Kayla said, looking up from her notes. She noticed Ryan was holding something in his hand.

"Not so fast," Ryan said, but his voice had suddenly changed into a high-pitched whine. "We have to do some research on that kid." He stepped out into the hall, leading the way to his private office.

There, he closed the door behind Kayla and held up the object he'd found. It was a *Daily Planet* note pad that he had stolen from Jimmy's jacket. "He had this in his pocket," Ryan said. "I think he's hiding something."

Kayla tried not to laugh as Ryan pulled off his wig and fake beard. *He looks so ridiculous without his disguise,* she thought. *I don't know why he doesn't just keep it on all the time!*

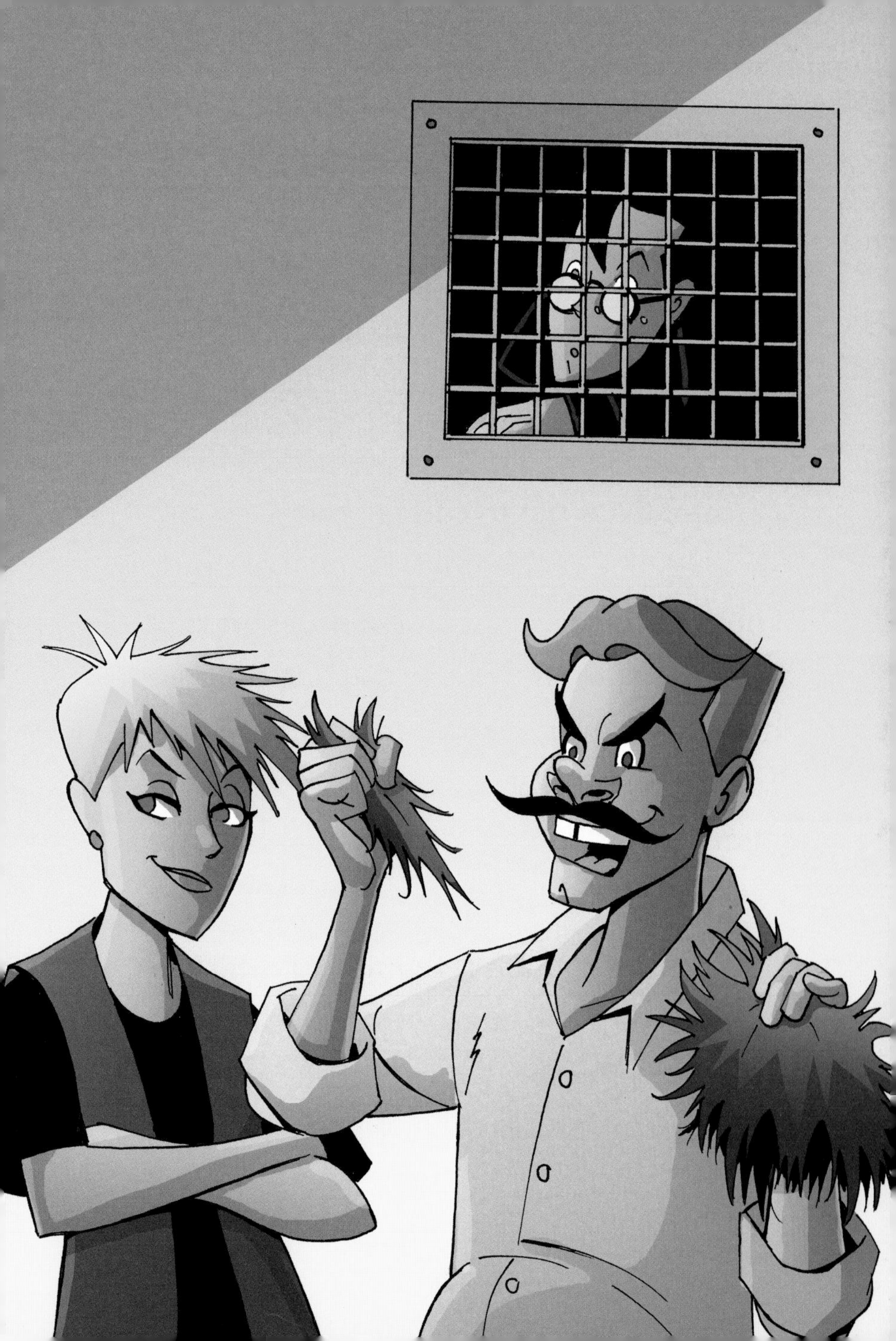

Alex then removed his false teeth, revealing himself as the gap-toothed Oswald Loomis.

"Maybe he just wants to look good on TV," Kayla said with a laugh. "Just like you, Prankie!"

"I told you not to call me that!" Loomis shouted. Before he could go on, there was a knock at the glass door. It was the burglar from the auto showroom, the one that had gotten away. Grinning, the Prankster opened it and reached out to shake the man's hand. The thief took a step back and shook his head.

"Oh no, you don't, Prankster!" said the burglar. "The last time we shook hands, I got an electric shock! I won't fall for that trick again."

The goofy-looking man held up his open palms. "Relax, Pug," he said. "See? No joy buzzer! C'mon, shake!"

Pug shrugged. He extended his arm and shook the Prankster's hand.

SPLASH! Instead of an electric shock, he got a face full of water from the Prankster's squirt gun. Kayla giggled as Pug wiped off his face.

"Thanks," Pug said angrily. "Now I don't feel so bad about telling you that I don't have your money."

No one in the room noticed it, but above their heads, Jimmy Olsen was listening. He had removed the screw from the grate of the vent, and squeezed inside. Then, he had crawled through the duct in the direction of Pug's voice.

"Not my problem," the Prankster replied. His voice was cold and menacing. "You know the rules. I had those kids dig that tunnel and install that pipe in it. They thought it was part of a prank, but it was really your entrance and escape route. For that, you owe me."

Jimmy had heard about the robbery, and he was starting to figure out what the Prankster was planning.

"All you had to do was dig a little more and cut a hole in the wall," the Prankster said. "It's not my fault you messed up."

The Prankster shoved Pug out of the office. "You've got until noon tomorrow to come up with the cash," he snarled. "Or else . . . .!"

CLINK CLANK!

"Did you hear something?" asked the Prankster.

"I think it came from above," said Kayla.

The Prankster looked up toward the faint noise. Jimmy held his breath. He had dropped his phone, which he'd been using to record the conversation.

Jimmy grabbed his phone and started crawling away as fast as he could, but the phone's light had gone out. He was in total darkness now.

ZWWWOOOOMMMM! Suddenly, Jimmy was sliding down a steeply-angled vent. Then he crashed through a grate and landed with a thud in the middle of a storage room. He looked up to see walls lined with shelves of DVDs.

The DVDs were recorded episodes of *Gotcha!* Then, Jimmy's eye caught something very strange. An entire row was labeled "Not For Airing."

Now Jimmy was sure he'd found the evidence that would prove Clark's theory.

CHAPTER 4

BART GETS THE GOODS

Back at the Daily Planet Building, Perry, Lois, Clark, and Jimmy were once again gathered around a TV monitor. But this time, they were watching several DVDs Jimmy had smuggled out of the *Gotcha!* offices after everyone had left.

"I practically had to stay there all night to make sure I could escape without being seen," Jimmy said, "but it was worth it."

The show on the screen was one of the "Not For Airing" episodes.

The episode was about kids digging a tunnel. The victim of the prank was told that the tunnel would help him sneak under a fence to an amusement park. The trick was that it led nowhere.

"So that's how the robbers got into the car dealership," Lois said.

"Exactly," said Clark. "Lieutenant Valens told me the police found the tunnel when Pug got away. They had no idea where it came from."

Lois pointed to the monitor. "They would have known, if this show had aired," she said. "People could make a connection between the crime and *Gotcha!*"

"No wonder Superman couldn't spot the third robber," Perry said. "That pipe must've been made of lead."

"Superman's X-ray vision wouldn't have been able to see through it," Jimmy said. "You guys will have to figure out the rest of it without me. I've got to get back to the studio."

"Jimmy," Lois said worriedly, "you came this close to being caught in that air duct. You've done some great work so far, but —"

Jimmy cut her off. "Yes, Miss Lane," he said, flashing his best smile. "And if I ever need another mom, I'll know where to find you!" With that, he dashed out of the office before anyone could say another word.

Perry shook his head. "Maybe that kid's got what it takes, after all," he said. Clark and Lois looked surprised. "But if you tell him I said so, you're fired."

"No worries, Perry," Lois said.

"The kids don't commit any crimes," Lois explained. "They help set them up."

Suddenly, the phone rang. Lois picked it up and sat down at her desk.

"That's crazy!" Perry said. "Why would anyone go to all that trouble? Why wouldn't Loomis just do the jobs himself?"

Clark smiled. "You said it yourself, Chief," he said. "Loomis is crazy. He's one of those 'theme criminals.' His crimes always have to involve a prank!"

Clark knew it was time for Superman to get involved. "If you'll excuse me, Chief," Clark said, "I have a different story to finish writing."

As Clark left, Lois put down the phone. "That was Lieutenant Valens. She wanted to thank you for the copies of those DVDs."

Lois rushed toward the door. "She's on her way to the studio now with an arrest warrant," Lois added. "Let's go!"

*   *   *

By the time Lois arrived at the *Gotcha!* offices with her video camera, Superman was standing with the police in front of the empty, two-story building.

"What's going on?" asked Lois as she raced up to Superman.

"Somehow they figured out we were on to them," said Lieutenant Valens.

"I've checked out the whole place," Superman said grimly, "and it's empty."

Lois's eyes widened with worry.

"That's right, Lois," Superman said. "There's no sign of Jimmy, either."

CHAPTER 5

THE BIG BANG

The Prankster had captured Jimmy Olsen, and there was nothing the teen could do about it. After removing his disguise, the crook handcuffed Jimmy in the back seat of his car.

Kayla was driving them down an alley in a bad part of town. They were almost at their destination, the rear entrance to an run-down building.

"This morning, we saw the mess you left downstairs," the Prankster snarled. "This is your chance to talk!"

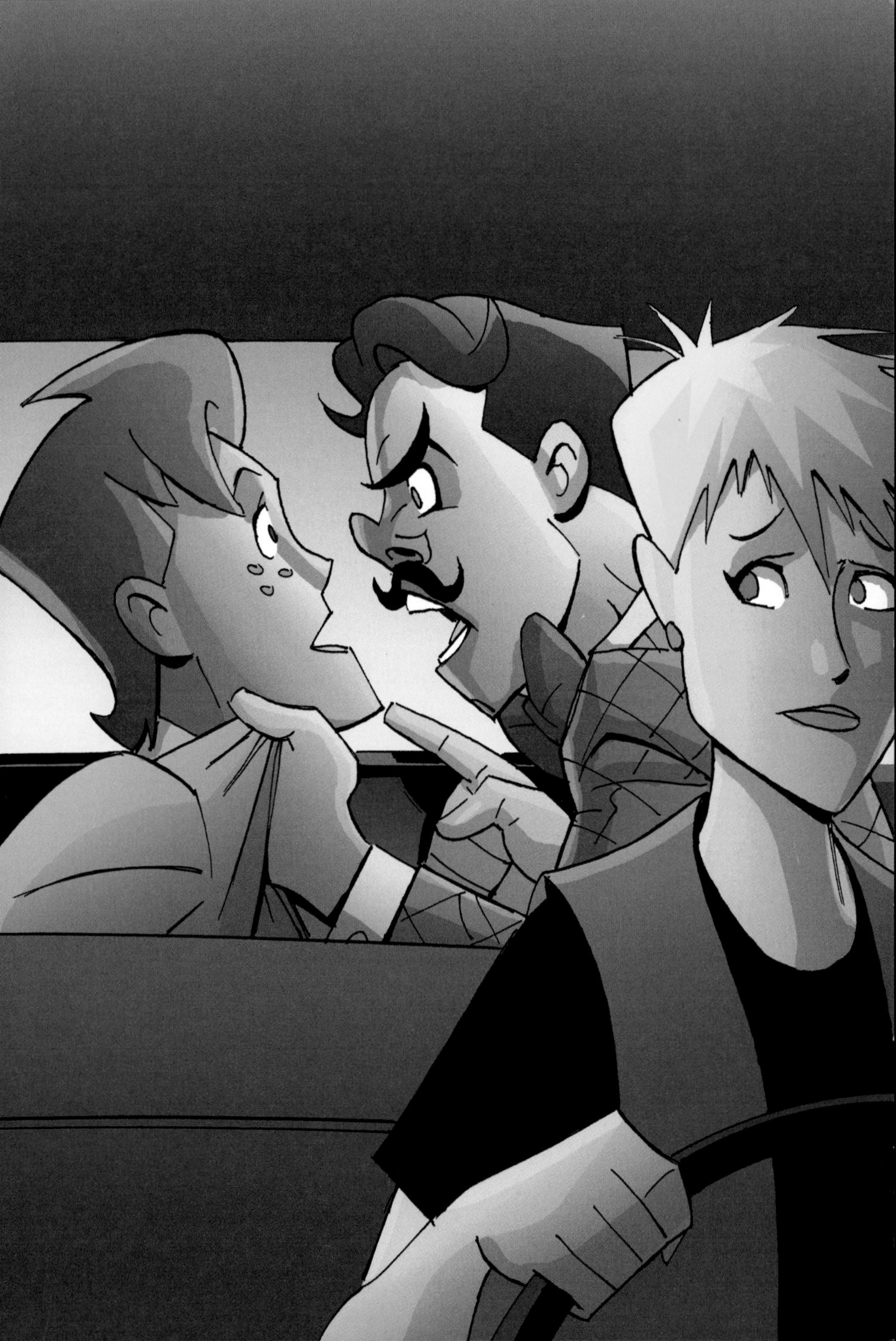

"Someone has been helping themselves to our DVD collection," the Prankster said.

Jimmy said nothing. He just continued what he'd been doing since the Prankster had handcuffed him. He was doing it very, very slowly, so no one would notice. He was moving his right hand toward his left.

"Somebody removed the grate over an air duct, too," the Prankster said, holding up a large screw. "But they forgot to replace all the bolts."

Jimmy winced. He thought he'd been so careful. Lois and Clark were right. Undercover work is dangerous unless you know exactly what you're doing.

"We never had trouble like that before you came along," the Prankster screamed. "Who are you? What do you want?"

Finally Jimmy was able to reach the button on the side of his wristwatch. It made a special sound, a high-frequency distress call that only Superman could hear.

Back at the empty warehouse, Lois was busy interviewing Lieutenant Valens on her video camera.

THWOOOOMMM!!

They turned to see Superman fly straight up in the air. They couldn't know, however, that the Prankster had glanced down just as Jimmy pushed the button. Now he tore the watch off Jimmy's wrist and smashed it against the car door.

The Prankster was beginning to get it. "The *Daily Planet* note pad, the watch . . . ! You're Superman's friend, Jimmy Olsen!"

Jimmy gulped.

By now, Jimmy had been led to the open doorway of a dark warehouse. The daylight from the alley didn't let him see much. He could barely make out piles of shipping crates and bubble wrap. There were also stacks of boxes filled with unsold novelties, like decks of marked playing cards and trick coins.

The Prankster pointed to the floor at what looked like several scattered pillows. "You've heard of whoopee cushions?"

The Prankster grinned as he took a screw out of his pocket. "Well, check this out!" The Prankster tossed the screw onto one of the pillows.

The "whoopee cushion" exploded with the force of a hand grenade!

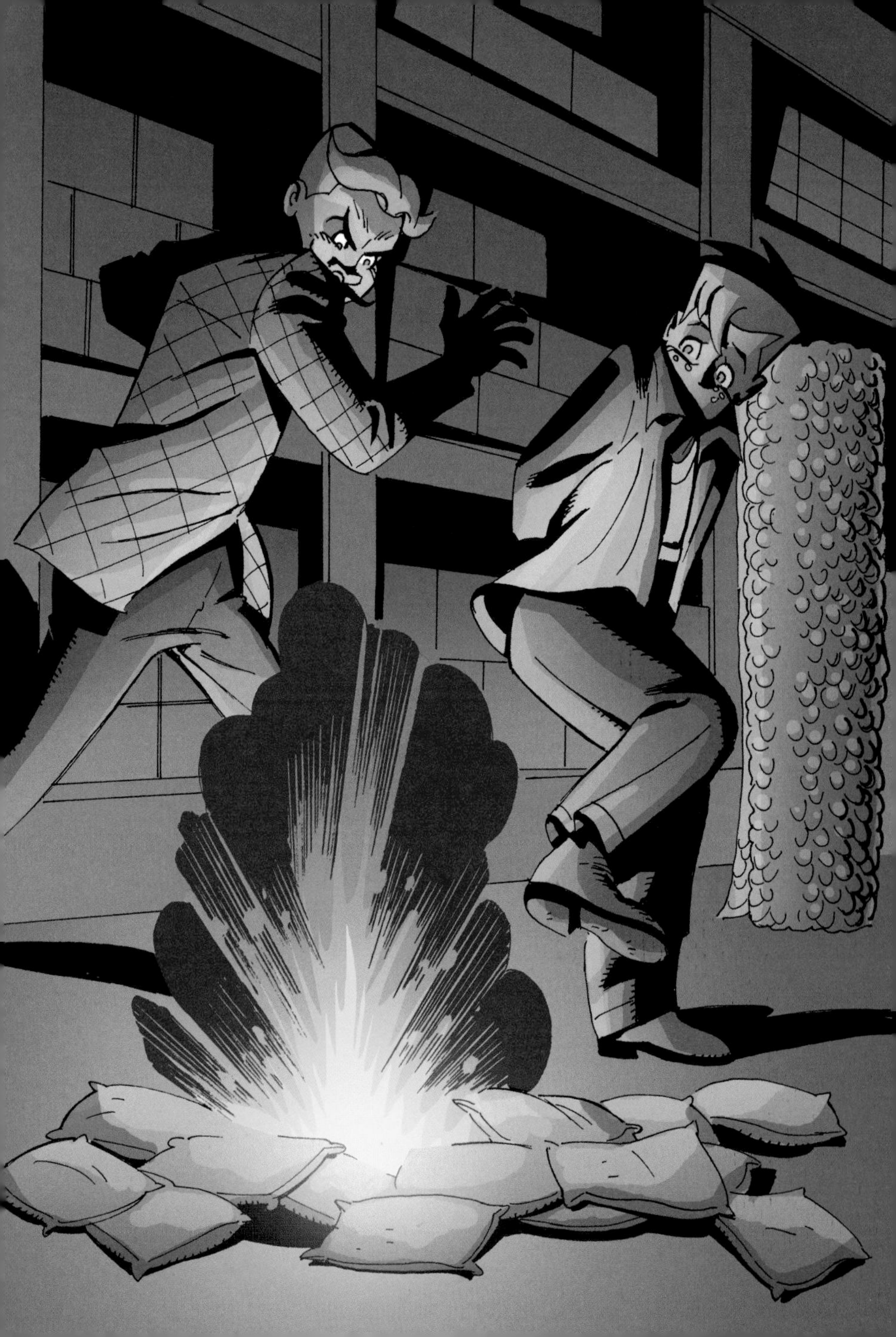

The Prankster chuckled nastily. "Here, every day is April Fool's Day," he said. "I store all my cleverest inventions here."

Then the Prankster started blindfolding Jimmy with his handkerchief. The teenager tried to act brave. As everything went dark, however, Jimmy knew he was in serious trouble.

*   *   *

Superman landed back at the studio. "Jimmy's signal stopped before I could track it down," he told Lois.

Lois seemed confused. "Can't you use your super-vision to find him?"

But before Superman could reply, Lois added, "In a city this size, though, where would you even start?"

"I may have an idea," Superman said.

Superman pointed to Lois's video camera, still in her hand. "Rewind your video, and play it again, Lois."

Lois did as Superman asked. The video's sound told the Man of Steel how far away Jimmy was when he sent the signal and in which direction. In seconds, he was rocketing toward the Metropolis warehouse district. With his super-vision, he scanned every run-down building and storefront below him.

*   *   *

Meanwhile, back in the warehouse, the Prankster gave Jimmy a rough shove. The teen stumbled forward, stepping closer and closer to the exploding pillows. Between the handcuffs and the blindfold, Jimmy could barely keep his balance. He had no idea where he was headed.

ZWWWOOOOMMMM!

He heard a familiar sound of rushing wind and thought the crooks had run away.

He turned in what he thought was their direction. Jimmy didn't realize he was about to step on one of the explosive cushions.

Just as his foot was lowering down on top of a pillow, he felt a hand grab his ankle. Another hand gripped his wrists. **FWOOSHHHHH!!** He was being lifted into the air!

"Superman!" he cried.

The Man of Steel set him down safely in the packing and shipping area, far from the deadly pillows. "Thanks, big guy!" Jimmy said.

"No problem, Jimmy," Superman said as he removed Jimmy's blindfold and handcuffs. "Or, should I call you Bart?"

Jimmy frowned. "Are you making fun of me, Superman?" he asked.

"No, not at all," Superman reassured him. "You did some great work out there, kid. You're a natural reporter."

Jimmy smiled shyly. "Wow, thanks!" he said.

"Just promise me one thing," Superman added. "Be a little more careful next time."

When he was free of his restraints, Jimmy called the police on his cell phone.

"Wait here, Jimmy," Superman said. "The Prankster's unpredictable, so until the police arrive, we'll have to be cautious."

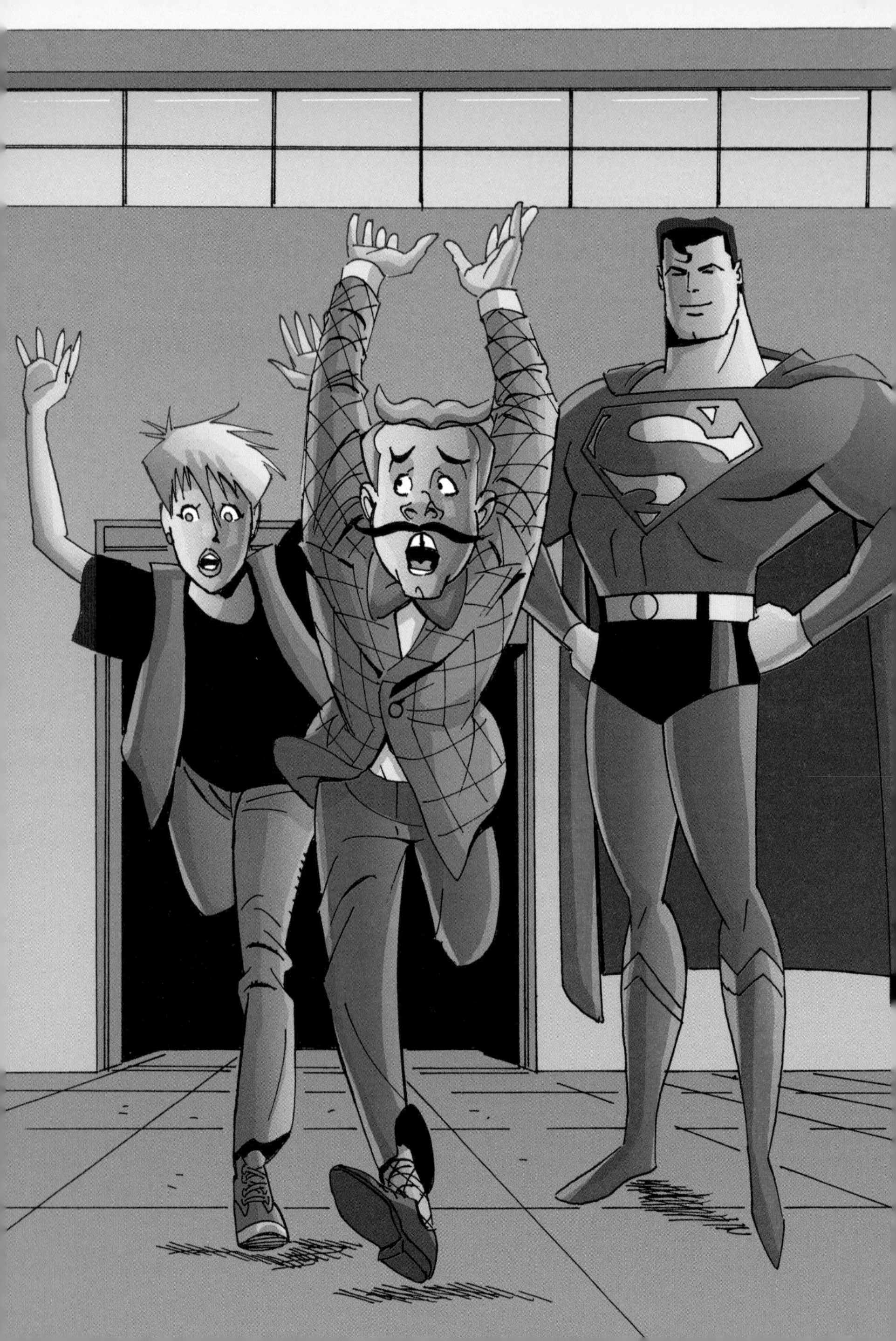

In the alley, the Prankster and Kayla had almost made it to their car when Superman appeared in front of them. He was standing in their path and blocking their escape. They heard the sound of approaching police sirens. Quickly, they turned and ran back toward the warehouse.

Suddenly, the two crooks came running frantically back into the alley. They held their hands above their heads.

"Don't shoot, don't shoot, we give up!" they cried out to Superman. "Please don't let the police shoot us!"

Superman quickly grabbed the two criminals. As he led them away, the Man of Steel smiled from ear to ear.

"What's so funny?" The Prankster asked.

Just then, the Prankster heard the sound of sirens growing louder.

"The police haven't even arrived yet," Superman said. He nodded at Jimmy, who was standing in the doorway.

Jimmy held a sheet of plastic bubble wrap used for packing. He popped a few, giggling at the Prankster. BANG! BANG!

For once, the victim of a prank was the Prankster himself!

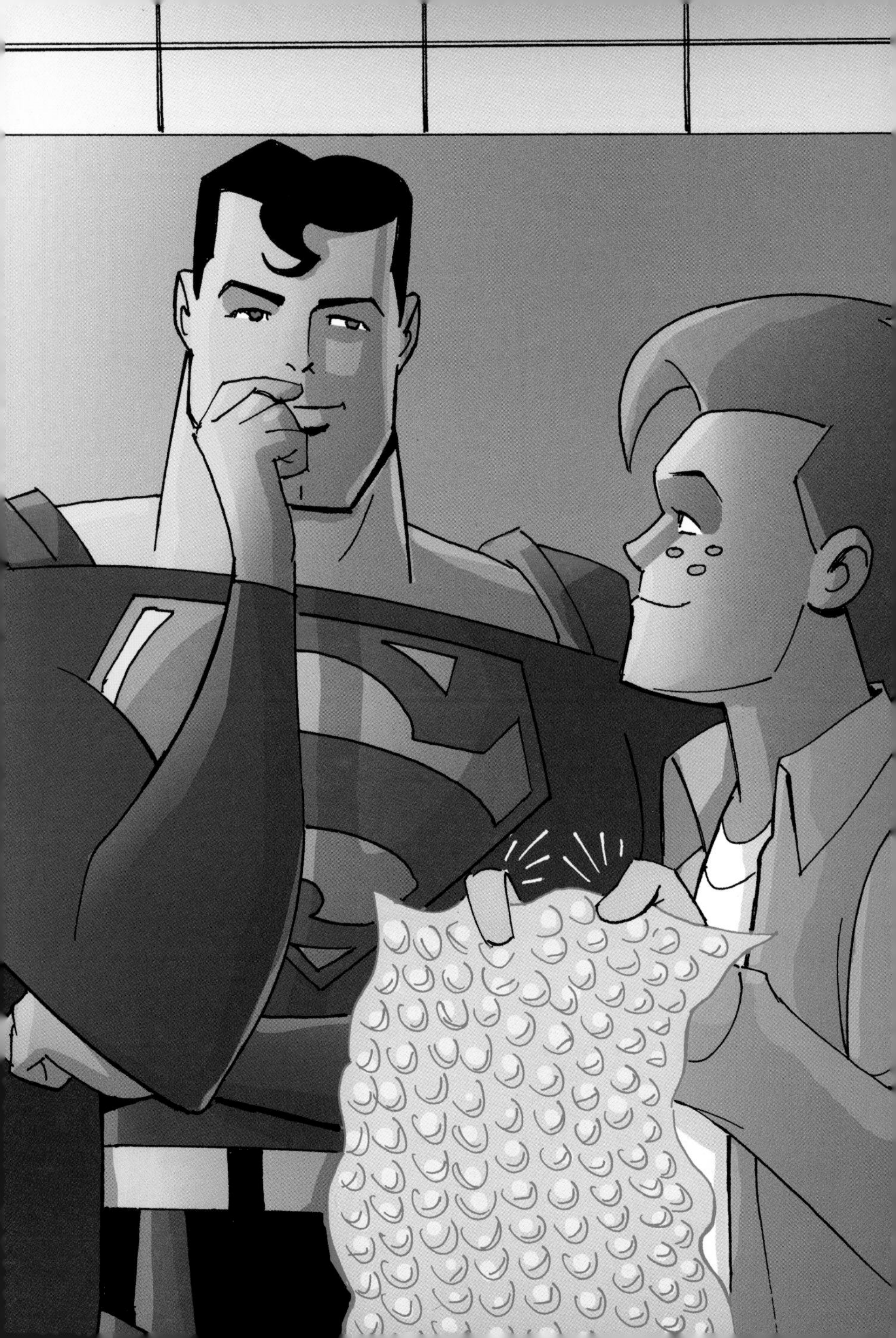

DAILY PLANET

WHO IS THE PRANKSTER?

Oswald Loomis once led a happy, laugh-filled life as the host of a popular children's TV show. He told jokes, made kids giggle, and had plenty of cash. But when the powers that be decided to ax Oswald's show, he went crazy — and vowed to take Metropolis's citizens down with him. As the Prankster, he plays deadly gags, with only the Man of Steel standing between him and madness. The Prankster may be a clown, but he's no joke — this crazy trickster is looking to make a fool out of the Man of Steel.

- The Prankster uses a variety of deadly gags to distract and incapacitate his victims. He created a device that makes people giggle uncontrollably so he can steal people's belongings while they're doubled over in laughter. He also uses electric joy buzzers and exploding whoopee cushions in his comical capers.

- Rather than commit crimes himself, the Prankster is instead paid by criminals to distract Superman with his pranks. That way, the crooks can commit crimes without the Man of Steel around to stop them.

- The Prankster once managed to trademark the English language! He then forced anyone who spoke or wrote in English to pay him by the word. Since Loomis hadn't broken the law, Superman couldn't do anything to stop him — until he found out that Oswald had bribed an official to get his patent.

- Loomis owns a gag store called Uncle Oley's Sure Fire Joke Shop. It appears to be a normal magic and joke store, but a hidden trap door leads to a high-tech underground base where the Prankster plans all his crimes.

BIOGRAPHIES

Martin Pasko has been working as a writer and editor in comics and television for many years, working on shows such as *Roseanne*, *The Twilight Zone*, and *Max Headroom*. Pasko has helped translate many comics into television series, including *Batman: The Animated Series*, for which he won a 1993 Daytime Emmy. He has also written Superman in many media, including TV animation and webisodes, as well as comics. He lives outside Manhattan with his wife, Judith, and their daughter, Laura.

Rick Burchett has worked as a comics artist for over 25 years. He has received the comics industry's Eisner Award three times, Spain's Haxtur Award, and he has been nominated for England's Eagle award. Rick lives with his wife and two sons near St. Louis, Missouri.

Lee Loughridge has been working in comics for more than fifteen years. He currently lives in sunny California in a tent on the beach.

GLOSSARY

cautious (KAW-shuhss)—if you are cautious, you try to avoid mistakes or danger

disguise (diss-GIZE)—conceal or hide something

distress (diss-TRESS)—in need of help

evidence (EV-uh-duhnss)—information and facts that help prove something

faint (FAYNT)—hard to hear or barely noticeable

grim (GRIM)—gloomy, stern, and unpleasant

menacing (MEN-uhss-ing)—threatening or dangerous

panicked (PAN-ikd)—felt great terror or fright

reassured (ree-uh-SHURD)—comforted someone, or convinced them to think positively

restraints (ri-STRAYNTZ)—handcuffs, or something used to hold someone still

scattered (SKAT-urd)—spread over a wide area

winced (WINSSD)—flinched or shrank back because of pain, fear, or embarrassment

DISCUSSION QUESTIONS

1. Jimmy Olsen goes undercover to help solve a crime. Is it ever okay to lie about who you are? Why or why not?

2. The Prankster has his own television show. What do you think is the best show on TV?

3. This book has ten illustrations. Which one is your favorite? Why?

WRITING PROMPTS

1. The Prankster likes to play practical jokes. Have you ever been tricked? Have you pulled pranks on others? Write about it.

2. Superman uses several of his superpowers to fight crime. Imagine that you're a super hero. What is your name? What superpowers do you have? Write about it. Then draw a picture of yourself as a super hero.

3. Clark Kent has two jobs — being a super hero, and as a reporter at the *Daily Planet*. What do you want to do for a living? Write about your perfect job.

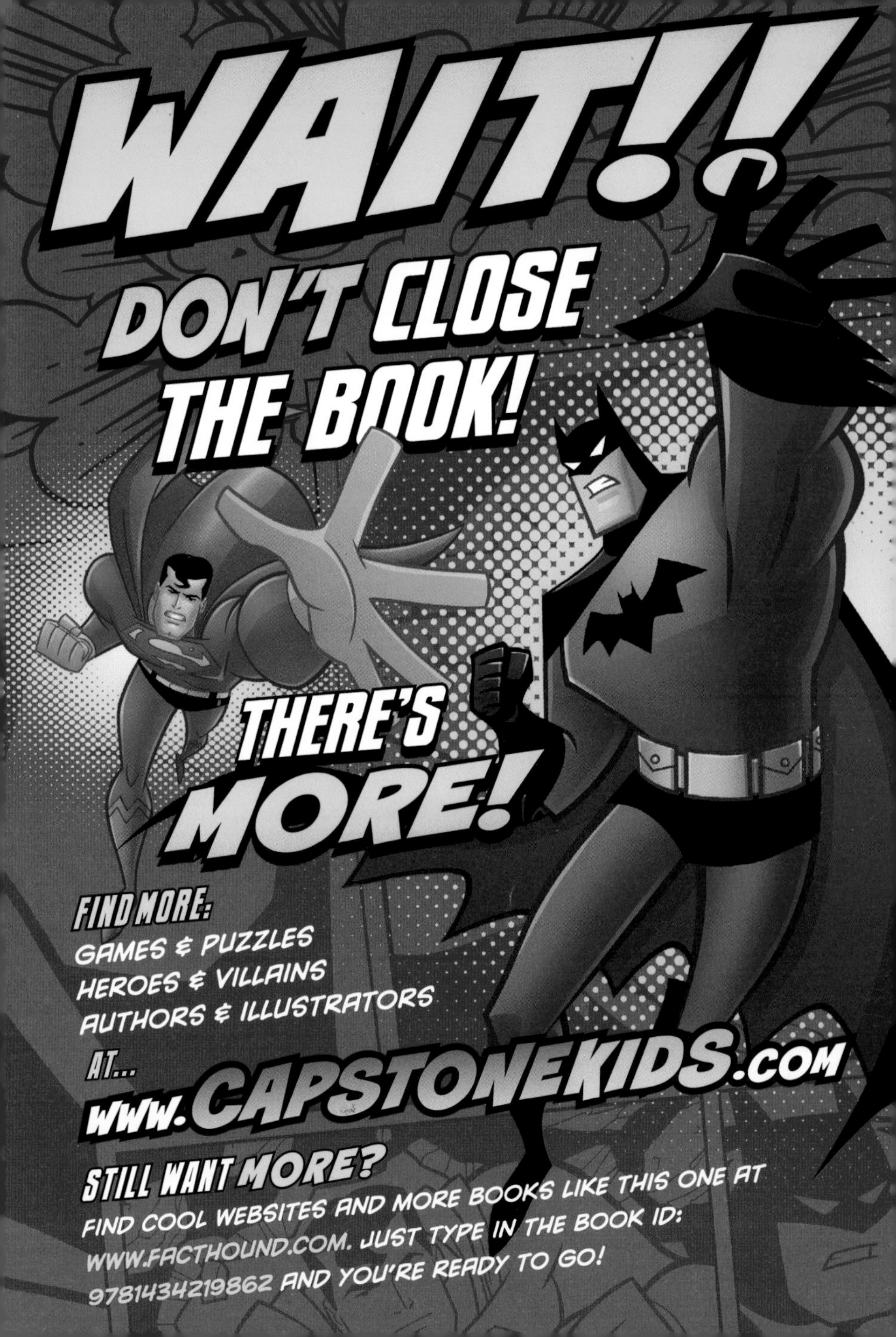
WAIT!!
DON'T CLOSE THE BOOK!
THERE'S MORE!
FIND MORE:
GAMES & PUZZLES
HEROES & VILLAINS
AUTHORS & ILLUSTRATORS
AT...
WWW.CAPSTONEKIDS.COM
STILL WANT MORE?
FIND COOL WEBSITES AND MORE BOOKS LIKE THIS ONE AT
WWW.FACTHOUND.COM. JUST TYPE IN THE BOOK ID:
9781434219862 AND YOU'RE READY TO GO!

MORE NEW SUPERMAN ADVENTURES!

COSMIC BOUNTY HUNTER

DEEP SPACE HIJACK

PARASITE'S POWER DRAIN

THE DEADLY DREAM MACHINE

THE SHADOW MASTERS

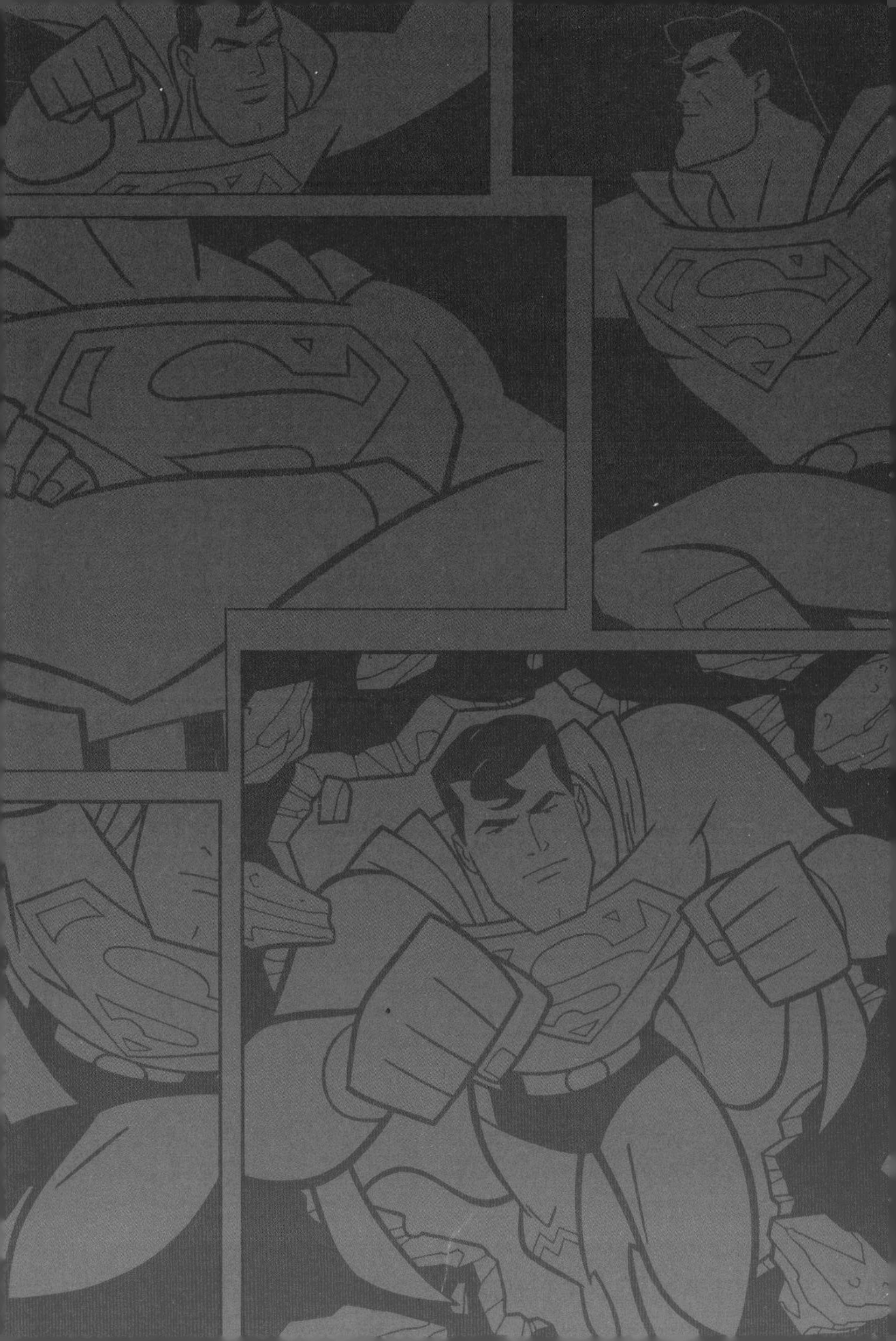

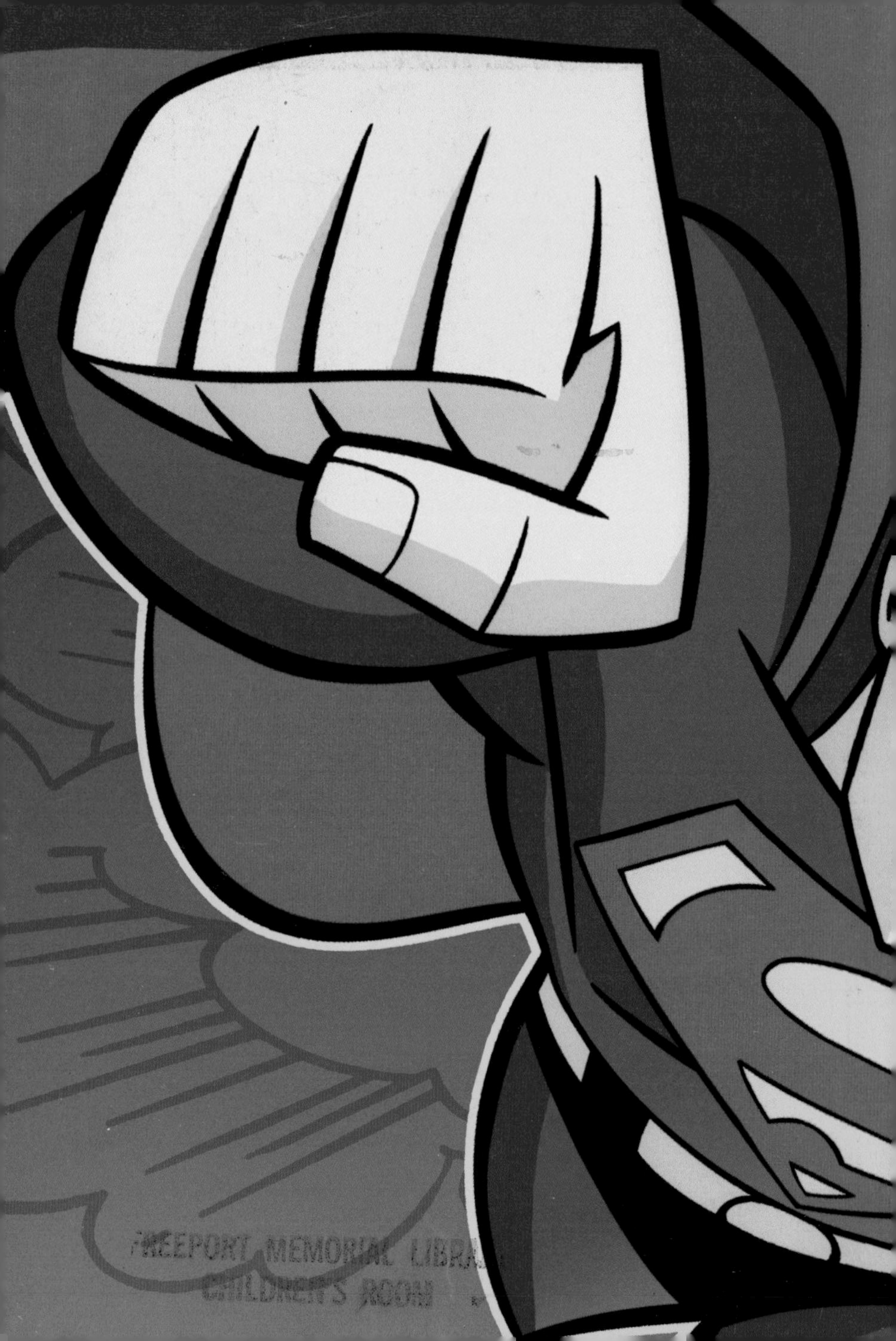